WAJHA

VOL 1

SUMANT GUPTA

Made with ♥ on the Notion Press Platform
www.notionpress.com

To the curious minds that never stop asking,
and to the brave hearts that chase the truth—even when
it's buried deep in shadows.

This story is for those who believe that every silence
hides a clue,
every glance holds a secret,
and every action has a wajha—a reason.

To the ones who trust their instincts when the world calls
them paranoid,
and to the seekers who know that behind every crime,
every lie, every twist—
there is always something more.

You are not just readers.
You are detectives, believers, and witnesses.

Welcome to the chase.
The reason you're looking for... is waiting.

Contents

Preface

Every story has a beginning.
But some don't begin with love, or light, or laughter.
Some begin with silence. With questions. With fear.
Wajha Vol 1 is one of those stories.

This is not just a tale of murder or mystery.
It is a journey through shadows—where every step forward
uncovers something hidden behind.
A web of secrets spun carefully, and lies told so
convincingly, they almost became the truth.
But in every deception lies a purpose, a motive, a reason.
A wajha.

In a world where trust is fragile and truth is layered,
this story follows those who dare to pull the thread—
even if it unravels everything.

So turn the page,
but read carefully.
Nothing here is without reason.
Not the silence. Not the screams. Not even the dead.

Foreword

When I first heard the word Wajha—meaning reason—it lingered with me.
Because in every story, and more importantly, in every crime, there is always a reason.
Not always visible. Not always justifiable.
But always there.

Wajha Vol 1 was born out of this very obsession.
Not with violence, but with the why behind it.
What pushes a person to the edge?
What turns love into vengeance, friendship into betrayal, or silence into a scream?

This isn't just another murder mystery.
It is a layered exploration of people, motives, and masks—
a story where everyone has something to hide, and yet, everything leads back to a singular truth.

As you step into these pages, I invite you to do more than just follow the clues.
Feel the tension. Question the intentions. Doubt every certainty.
Because in this story, answers are not handed to you.
You have to earn them.

Welcome to a world where truth is slippery, danger is quiet,
and the reason... is everything.
— Sumant Gupta

Acknowledgements

Writing Wajha Vol 1 has been both a journey and a challenge—one that wouldn't have been possible without the support of so many remarkable people.

First and foremost, I owe my deepest gratitude to my family. Their unwavering belief in me, even when the nights were long and the story seemed to have no end, gave me the strength to keep writing. To my loved ones who have patiently listened to my ideas, debated plot twists, and offered their advice with love, thank you for being my pillars.

A special thanks to my beta readers—[Neha Gupta], whose sharp minds and honest feedback challenged me to dig deeper into the mysteries within these pages. You pushed me to unravel the layers of the plot, to breathe life into the characters, and to create the suspense that drives this story forward.

To those who inspired the world of Wajha Vol 1, I am forever grateful. The shadowy corners of our reality, the unspoken motives, and the untrustworthy faces are a reflection of the complexity of human nature. This book is for the questioners, the doubters, and the seekers of truth.

And lastly, to the readers—thank you for choosing to walk this twisted path with me. Every word you read, every clue you uncover, and every twist you follow is a shared experience. This story is yours as much as it is mine.

I hope you find what you're looking for.

Prologue

The city was asleep.

Or at least, it seemed that way. Beneath the heavy veil of the night, every shadow seemed to whisper a secret, and every corner held its breath. But not all was quiet.

Inspector Suresh stood in the darkened alley, the cold air biting at his skin. The crime scene before him was unsettlingly still, as if the universe itself had frozen in time. A man lay sprawled across the ground, his eyes wide open in shock, his last breath still lingering in the air. But it wasn't just the body that unnerved Suresh. It was the story it told—one that didn't quite add up.

The victim, a well-known journalist, had no apparent enemies. His life had seemed ordinary, until that one moment when he was found dead under mysterious circumstances. A man's death is never simple, especially when the fingerprints don't match, and the clues don't fit the puzzle.

But what was most troubling wasn't the fact of the murder.

It was the note found beside him, written in a scrawl that only one person could have left.

The reason is here. Seek the truth.

The words rang in Suresh's mind, heavy with meaning. This wasn't just a murder.

It was the beginning of something much larger.

Across the city, in a quiet apartment, Rudra sat alone, his fingers trembling over the pages of a new manuscript. His latest book—a chilling thriller about a string of murders—was nearly finished. He had always drawn inspiration from the world around him, but this time, his pen had become far too prophetic.

The lines between his story and reality were blurring.

Somewhere in the distance, a siren wailed. The city was waking up to something dark and dangerous.

And Rudra, the author whose words seemed to predict death, had no idea that the game he had set in motion was just beginning.

Chapter 1: The First Murder

October 12, 2021 – Around 8:30 PM

The highway that cut through the outskirts of the city was oddly silent that night. No blaring horns, no screeching brakes. Just the soft whisper of wind skimming across the asphalt and the faint crackle of the patrol car's old radio, playing Kishore Kumar's "Neele Neele Ambar Par." The melody floated into the night, a nostalgic tune trying to mask the unease hanging in the air.

Inside the patrol vehicle, Inspector Suresh sat stiffly. It wasn't his usual beat. Normally, he delegated these late-night rounds to his juniors. But tonight, something had gnawed at him—a restlessness that refused to be reasoned with. He'd told himself it was just insomnia. But somewhere deep inside, he knew better.

The constable beside him cracked a joke about how the ghosts must be out partying in the silence, but Suresh barely smiled. His eyes were glued to the road, scanning the shadows.

Then it happened.

"Sir! That car over there!" the constable suddenly yelled, jolting forward and pointing to the right side of the road.

Suresh's heart lurched. He turned sharply to look—and there it was. A black luxury SUV, half-tilted off the roadside embankment, its headlights still on, engine off, and the driver's side door slightly ajar.

They sped toward it, the cruiser's tires spitting gravel. Something about the scene felt... wrong. Not just the accident, but the stillness around it. The air itself seemed to hold its breath.

As Suresh yanked open the door, the sickening smell of blood hit him first—coppery, thick, unmistakable. What he saw inside made the hair on the back of his neck stand up.

Aryan Sharma.

The bratty, arrogant son of MLA Shyamveer Sharma. Known more for scandals than substance. Known for breaking laws like they were glass toys. But now... now he was broken himself.

Dead.

His body slumped awkwardly, like a discarded doll. Eyes wide open. Lifeless. But that wasn't the worst of it.

Not even close.

When the forensic team arrived minutes later, one of the junior officers began retching. The senior forensic expert, an older man who'd seen more corpses than birthday cakes, stepped back after the examination, his face pale.

"Sir... he was raped. Before being killed."

The word rape felt like a punch to the gut. For a moment, no one moved. No one breathed.

Suresh clenched his fists. Murder was one thing. But this... this was depraved. A message, not a crime. And that message was personal.

He pulled out his phone with trembling hands and dialed the Commissioner.

"This is Suresh. We have a problem."

By the time the media got wind of it, chaos had erupted. The highway was swarmed—reporters yelling into mics, cameramen shoving past barricades, drones buzzing overhead. News vans lined the road like a sick parade. BREAKING: MLA'S SON FOUND MURDERED IN MYSTERIOUS CIRCUMSTANCES.

Aryan's body was transported under heavy police escort, lights flashing as if to fend off the darkness of what had just begun.

At the Sharma residence, grief turned into a scene from a tragedy.

Aryan's mother collapsed onto the marble floor, screaming, clawing at her sari, her voice echoing through the grand halls. No one could comfort her. No one dared.

MLA Shyamveer Sharma stood in the center of the room, motionless. His eyes locked on his son's body like they could will it back to life. But they couldn't. And he knew it.

He didn't cry.

He didn't speak.

Not until the silence was unbearable.

"The last rites," he said coldly, voice like gravel. "Tomorrow. 9 AM sharp. Call everyone."

October 13, 9:00 AM

The cremation ground felt like a stage set for a political opera. Black cars. White kurta-pajamas. Sunglasses hiding calculating eyes. Whispers flew like flies—Was it revenge? Was it a setup? Who would dare touch the son of an MLA?

The MLA arrived last, flanked by bodyguards, his bulletproof car creeping forward like a tank in enemy territory. He stepped out and stared at the pyre as if daring the fire to blink first.

Inspector Suresh, standing among the gathered officers, finally moved forward.

"Sir, I want this case," he said to the Commissioner, voice firm.

The Commissioner turned, studied his face. "Good. I was going to hand it to you anyway."

"You were?" Suresh raised an eyebrow.

"There's no other officer who can handle this mess," the Commissioner said, his smile barely a twitch. "Not without losing their job... or their life. Go get 'em, my boy."

The flames crackled to life behind them. Aryan's body turned to smoke, and the case turned into war.

Later, as the crowd thinned, MLA Sharma walked over to the Commissioner. They spoke in murmurs, low enough to be drowned out by the fire.

When Sharma left—still silent, still deadly—Suresh stepped closer.

"What did he say?"

The Commissioner looked at him with the weariness of a man caught between justice and politics.

"He gave us a one-month deadline."

Suresh frowned. "And if we fail?"

The Commissioner exhaled, a cloud of breath heavy with implications.

"If we don't catch whoever did this... he will."

CHAPTER 2: THE SECOND MURDER

The glittering chandeliers of Hotel Velour cast soft, opulent light on the city's elite. Crystal glasses clinked, designer perfumes mingled with wine, and conversations flowed as elegantly as the jazz humming in the background. Tonight was a celebration—not of politics or power—but of prose.

The guest of honor? Rudra Ahuja.

A literary heartthrob. Known for tales soaked in rain-kissed romance and teary-eyed family sagas. But tonight, the crowd buzzed with anticipation because Rudra had done the unthinkable. He'd crossed genres.

From roses to razors.

From love to murder.

Inspector Suresh stood by the exit, hands folded behind his back, scanning the lounge with the sharp instincts of a man who'd seen too many masks in his life. Though dressed in formal civvies, his presence was unmistakably police. His eyes lingered on the high-profile guests—the business tycoons, politicians, influencers, and the occasional suspicious loner sipping too little and watching too much.

Security was tight. The Commissioner had insisted on it, considering the storm the first murder had stirred. Especially with Rudra's book series now eerily mirroring real-life headlines.

And Rudra? Nowhere to be seen.

Suresh checked his watch. Twenty minutes late.

Then the elevator dinged.

Out walked Rudra—tailored to perfection, a mischievous smile playing on his lips, and the confidence of a man who knew every eye would follow him. He stepped up to the stage, adjusted the mic with flair, and began.

"A very good evening to all of you wonderful, slightly disturbed people," he grinned, triggering a ripple of laughter.

"Thank you for showing so much love to my first and second episodes. You all know me—romantic Rudra, Mr. Drama. But this time... I wanted to write something that bled. Something that whispered danger. And guess what? You liked it. Which tells me... maybe I'm not the only twisted one in this room."

Another round of amused applause.

"So here's my promise—more episodes, faster. Bloodier. Deadlier. Hope you survive the ride."

He winked, stepped off the stage, and was immediately engulfed by fans and flashing cameras.

Later, while guests mingled over champagne and slow jazz, Suresh found himself standing beside Rudra.

"You're the cop everyone's whispering about," Rudra said, swirling his drink. "The one hunting Aryan Sharma's killer."

"And you're the writer everyone's reading about," Suresh replied. "The one romanticizing killers."

They both smiled. An odd pair—one fed on facts, the other on fiction. But for some reason, they clicked. Maybe it was the darkness they both sensed in each other—or maybe it was just mutual curiosity.

When the night drew to a close, Suresh offered to drop Rudra home.

"Most authors get stalkers," Rudra chuckled, stepping into the car. "I get a police escort. Not bad."

The city lights passed them in a blur of neon and shadow.

Later that night

The station was quiet when Suresh returned, the silence punctuated only by the creak of his chair and the low hum of the ancient ceiling fan.

He turned on the television, expecting cricket scores or late-night debates.

Instead, a breaking news banner screamed across the screen.

BREAKING: Another body found on NH-42, 30 kilometers from the city. Male. Brutally raped and murdered. Details disturbingly similar to the Aryan Sharma case.

Suresh didn't breathe for three seconds.

Then he was on his feet, keys in hand.

Ten minutes later, he was outside the Commissioner's house, banging on the door like a madman.

"What in God's name—" the Commissioner opened the door mid-sentence and froze at the look on Suresh's face.

"Another one," Suresh said simply. "Another boy. Same pattern."

They didn't speak during the drive. There was nothing left to say that the silence hadn't already screamed.

MLA Sharma's residence

The room was colder than it should've been. Not because of the air conditioning—but because of the man seated inside.

MLA Shyamveer Sharma stood before the giant LED screen, arms crossed, eyes locked on the news coverage. Rage radiated from him like heat from steel.

He didn't turn when they entered.

"You didn't come empty-handed, did you?" he asked without looking.

Suresh hesitated. "Unfortunately... we did, sir."

Sharma finally turned. His face was unreadable, but his voice cut like a scalpel.

"Same method?"

"Yes. A boy. Around the same age as Aryan. No ID yet, but... the similarities are undeniable."

Sharma sat down slowly, like a mountain folding in on itself. "Did Aryan know him?"

"We were hoping you could tell us."

"I knew all of Aryan's friends. That boy wasn't one of them."

The silence returned, more suffocating than before.

Suresh turned to the Commissioner. "This case... it's getting tangled instead of unraveling."

The MLA's gaze snapped back to him. "A week has passed, Inspector. You now have three weeks left."

He leaned forward, voice dropping to a threat wrapped in silk.

"After that... don't stop me. Because I won't stop myself."

Suresh adjusted his collar, spine straightening.

"Well, sir... stopping people is kind of our job."

He saluted.

"For now—Jai Hind."

Later that night – Commissioner's Residence

The Commissioner poured himself a drink. Suresh paced like a caged lion.

"This case is poison," Suresh muttered. "It's not just murder. It's personal. It's planned. And it's... taunting us."

"You think the killer's doing this to send a message?"

"I think he's building something. A narrative. Like chapters in a novel."

The Commissioner raised an eyebrow.

"Speaking of novels... Rudra?"

Suresh paused. "He's sharp. Plays dumb, but he's reading the room at all times. I don't think he's involved. But he knows the power of attention. And he's feeding on this case."

The Commissioner nodded. "Then we stop feeding it. Get to the crime scene. First thing tomorrow."

Suresh's jaw tightened. "Permission to head out at dawn?"

"Granted. Pack light."

Suresh picked up his coat.

The Commissioner's voice followed him as he opened the door.

"You're heading into darkness, Suresh."

Without turning, Suresh replied:

"I live there."

CHAPTER 3: THREADS OF BLOOD

Rajgaon – Crime Scene of the Second Murder

The dawn mist hung low over the outskirts of Rajgaon, wrapping the highway in a pale shroud like nature itself was trying to cover up what had happened. The blood had been washed away by last night's rain, but the stench of death lingered. It always did. Not in the air—but in memory.

Local constables stood around nervously, trying not to stare too hard at the dark stain on the asphalt or the broken bushes where the boy's body had been found. A few villagers lingered behind the barricades, murmuring superstitions under their breath.

Then came the screech of tires.

Inspector Suresh stepped out of the jeep like a force of nature. Dark glasses on. Shirt sleeves rolled up. Jaw clenched.

He didn't waste a second.

"Show me the perimeter. Who was first on the scene? I want the footage from every traffic camera between here and kilometer 35."

The officers scrambled, grateful for someone who sounded like he knew what he was doing. Suresh crouched near the ditch where the body had been dumped. His eyes scanned the area, tracing invisible threads—shoe prints, broken grass, tire marks that hadn't matched the official vehicles.

Something was wrong. No sign of a struggle. No signs of panic. Whoever did this had done it before.

This was ritual.

Elsewhere: The Hills of Gulmarg

Meanwhile, miles away, Police Commissioner Prakash Verma was traveling into the misty hills, where retirement met wisdom. He pulled into the sprawling farmhouse of Mr. Rajat .Singh, a legend among legends—former Police Commissioner, mentor, and the kind of man who still got phone calls when Delhi trembled.

Singh, now in his seventies, sat on his verandah sipping black tea, his eyes sharp despite his age.

"Sit down, Prakash," he said. "You look like hell."

"I feel worse," Verma muttered, taking the seat across from him.

Singh nodded. "Then let's talk murder."

Back in Rajgaon: The Second Victim's House

The home was small, humble, with peeling blue paint and flower pots clinging to the windows. Inside, grief was a living thing—thick, unspoken, choking.

Suresh entered slowly.

The victim's father sat cross-legged on a woven cot, staring at the wall. His hands trembled as he clasped a photo of his son.

"I'm sorry for your loss," Suresh began, gently.

The man nodded, eyes vacant. "He was just a boy…"

"I know. And I need your help. I promise we'll find whoever did this."

The man nodded again.

Suresh continued, "Your son… did he know Aryan Sharma?"

The man's face twitched. "Yes. They met once. A school trip to Goa. They stayed in touch after that. Some chats, maybe a video call here and there."

Suresh's heart rate spiked. There it was. A thread. Thin, but enough.

"Thank you," he said, then stood. "We'll get justice."

He walked out, his mind racing.

These boys weren't picked randomly. They were linked. And someone had planned this like a game of chess—every move in place before the board had even been set.

Local Police Station – Rajgaon

The walls were lined with old case files and dusty calendars. Suresh sat at a metal desk, connecting dots in silence.

Two boys. Goa. A connection.

He reached into his pocket and pulled out a folded notepad, writing a single line: "Pattern = Connection. Not chaos."

Then something clicked.

He bolted upright.

"Subedar!" he barked. "Start the engine! We're going back."

"Back where, sir?"

"To the beginning. And then to the Commissioner's house. I think I've got something."

Later That Evening – Commissioner Verma's Residence

The living room was dim, the air thick with tension. Commissioner Verma paced like a general before war. The door burst open, and in came Suresh, breathless, his face lit with adrenaline.

"Sir," he said. "We need to talk. I think I'm close to figuring this out."

"Good," Verma said. "Because I've got something to show you too. And it changes everything."

They sat.

Suresh laid out his findings: the Goa connection, the friendship between victims, the consistency in the killer's method.

Verma listened intently.

Then it was his turn.

"I visited Rajat Singh today," he began. "He's been watching this case closely."

Suresh raised an eyebrow. "He's retired."

"He's also the sharpest detective I've ever met."

Verma leaned forward, lowering his voice.

"He thinks the killer is Rudra Ahuja."

Suresh froze.

"The writer?"

Verma nodded.

"That doesn't make sense. Rudra's thriller series started after Aryan's murder. And the second killing happened only after he released Episode One."

"That's what I thought," Verma said. "Until Singh showed me this—"

He pulled out two manila envelopes and slid them across the table.

Suresh opened them. Inside were printed manuscripts—Rudra's next two unpublished episodes.

"How did he get these?"

"Let's just say Singh still has friends in the publishing world. The point is—look at the content."

Suresh scanned the pages.

His blood ran cold.

Every detail in the manuscript matched the crime scene. Even things not released to the press. The position of the body. The brand of cigarette found near the ditch. The message written in blood behind the thigh—a message Suresh had just discovered.

"How the hell does he know this?"

"That's what we have to find out," Verma said grimly.

"Either Rudra is scripting murders... or someone is following his writing like a rulebook."

They stared at each other, the realization settling in.

Three boys. Three brutal murders.

One charismatic author.

And a killer who may be hiding in plain sight.

Suresh closed the file slowly.

"This is no longer an investigation."

Verma nodded. "It's a countdown."

CHAPTER FOUR

EPISODE 4: UNRAVELING THE TRUTH

12:15 AM – Inspector Suresh's Apartment

A dim lamp flickered over Inspector Suresh's cluttered desk, casting long shadows on the walls. Papers were scattered, pens chewed dry, coffee gone cold. In his hand was a printout—Rudra's third story. His eyes scanned each line with surgical focus, but frustration clung to him like fog.

His phone buzzed.

Commissioner Verma: "Rudra has posted the third story. Looks like the fourth murder might happen soon. Read the story and meet me tomorrow. Goodnight."

Suresh rubbed his eyes, stretched his back, and clicked Download.

Outside, the world slept. Inside, death was still awake.

8:30 AM – Commissioner's Residence

Inspector Suresh looked like he hadn't slept a minute. Dark circles under his eyes, shirt hastily tucked in, files clutched under his arm. He knocked.

Commissioner Verma: "Come in!"

Suresh entered, sank into the sofa. Verma studied him for a moment, then spoke with calm authority.

Verma: "What happened, Suresh? Will you keep chewing your thoughts or spit them out?"

Suresh shook his head, exhaling heavily.

Suresh: "Sir, I read the third story all night. But... there's nothing new. It's just another rape and murder. Same formula. Same darkness. No specific details that connect it to the victims or crime scenes."

Verma leaned back, frowning.

Verma: "That's what we don't understand either. Singh Sahab believes Rudra is using these stories as a way to provoke us. And if we don't act fast... someone else will die."

Suresh: "So what do we do? Arrest him without proof?"

Verma: (after a pause) "No. Offer him protection. Tell Rudra he's in danger and we're assigning police security. Keep eyes on him. Every second. If he's not the killer... then the killer is watching him too."

Suresh: "And if he refuses?"

Verma: "Convince him. Or compel him. Either way, you've got my full backing."

12:00 PM – Outside Rudra's House

The police jeep screeched to a halt outside Rudra's upscale bungalow. A six-member unit stepped out, alert and armed. Suresh led the way to the door.

(Knock. Knock.)

Rudra: (opening the door with a smile) "Inspector! Welcome! I wasn't expecting—"

His words trailed off as he noticed the full team behind Suresh. His grin faltered.

Rudra: "What is this, sir? Has something happened?"

Suresh: "Let's talk inside."

They moved into the living room. Rudra sat on the edge of his sofa, nervous now.

Suresh: "Mr. Rudra, you've been assigned personal security. Headquarters believes your life is at risk."

Rudra: "What? My life? But... why? I don't have enemies. I'm just a writer!"

Suresh: "That's precisely why you're being watched. Someone's using your stories as inspiration. And until we find out who—it's our job to keep you safe."

Rudra: (incredulous) "So you think I'm innocent, yet you bring an entire battalion into my home?"

Suresh: "We're not sure of anything yet. But if you reject this security—we'll have no choice but to detain you under preventive custody."

Rudra: (laughs bitterly) "You're arresting me for writing fiction?"

Suresh: "I'm detaining you because four people are dead and you're the only common thread. You'll stay with us—safe, watched—for one week."

Rudra: (quietly) "This is a mistake. And you'll regret it."

Three Days Later – Midnight

It was eerily quiet. Rudra sat on the same couch he'd claimed three days ago, barely moving, barely speaking. The house had turned into a fortress.

Suresh's phone rang—an urgent call from one of his officers.

Officer: "Sir! Sir! A body's been found. Same highway. Same pattern. It's happened again!"

Suresh: "Where?!"

Officer: "The same place where MLA Sharma's son was murdered!"

The line went dead.

Suresh turned to Rudra, who stared at him with cold, unreadable eyes.

Rudra: "Satisfied now, Inspector? Or would you like another body to prove I'm not your killer?"

Suresh clenched his jaw. He couldn't reply. He didn't have to. He stormed out with the police unit.

3:30 AM – Crime Scene

Another young man. Dead. Raped. Thrown like garbage. No fingerprints. No witnesses. Just the same sickening precision.

Commissioner Verma: (on phone) "We messed up, Suresh. I messed up. We wasted time suspecting Rudra."

Suresh: "I'm at the scene. I'll send the body for postmortem. But sir—"

He paused, realization dawning like a cold splash of water.

Suresh: "The third and fourth victims... they were friends with Aryan. I just confirmed it. And the second victim too. They all knew each other."

There was silence on the other end.

Suresh: "Sir... these aren't random killings. They're not inspired by fiction. They're personal."

Verma: "So who's behind it?"

Suresh's voice dropped to a whisper.

Suresh: "The only person who knew all four boys. The one man who never shed a tear... but gave us a deadline."

Verma: "...MLA Sharma."

Suresh stood still under the moonlight, heart thudding.

The game had never been about catching a writer.

It was about unraveling a man with power—and a vendetta soaked in blood.

EPISODE 5: "THE SHOCKING REVELATION"

Inspector Suresh had been chasing the shadows of truth for days, trying to make sense of the gruesome series of murders that had left the city on edge. The investigation, which had once seemed straightforward, had spiraled into a maze of confusion and conflicting motives. Each new discovery seemed to open more doors to darkness, but none offered clear answers. It was a case that gnawed at his mind, and every step he took only seemed to lead to more questions.

The most unsettling part of it all, however, was the discovery that all the murdered boys were somehow connected. That single piece of information had changed everything. And now, the last connection—the one piece that might tie it all together—led him directly to MLA Sahab.

It was an unseasonably quiet afternoon when Suresh, weary from sleepless nights and endless leads, made his way to the mansion. The air felt heavy, like a storm was approaching—one that he couldn't predict, no matter how hard he tried. As he passed through the grand gates of MLA Sahab's estate, he couldn't shake the feeling that something was about to unfold, something that would forever change the course of the investigation—and possibly his life.

Suresh arrived at the study, where MLA Sahab was waiting for him. The usually confident politician looked anything but certain today. His expression was tight, his posture stiff. There was a kind of coldness in the room that sent a chill through Suresh. The grand room, with its tall bookshelves, antique furniture, and air of wealth, now felt oppressive.

As Suresh entered, the tense silence was broken by the MLA's voice. But it wasn't the booming, commanding tone that Suresh was used to. Instead, it was quiet, almost hesitant.

"Inspector," MLA Sahab said, looking up from his desk with a grave expression. "I've been thinking a lot about your investigation. There's something I need to tell you. It's a story that's been weighing on me for months, and I've never shared it with anyone. But perhaps it's time you knew."

Suresh's curiosity piqued. He took a seat across from the MLA, his instincts already sensing that this was the turning point of the investigation.

"Go on, sir," Suresh said, trying to keep his voice calm despite the growing anxiety in his chest.

MLA Sahab leaned back in his chair, his fingers tapping nervously against the polished wood of the desk. He looked down at his hands, almost as if trying to summon the words, before finally speaking in a low, almost confessional tone.

"A few months ago," the MLA began, his voice tinged with regret, "my son Aryan and his friends went on a trip to Goa. It was supposed to be a carefree holiday. The beach, the parties, the usual nonsense that boys their age get into. But there was one thing that happened—something that went unnoticed by everyone, even by me."

Suresh sat up straighter, sensing that the MLA was about to reveal something crucial.

"My son, along with his friends, made advances toward Rudra's wife," the MLA continued, his voice barely above a whisper. "It was wrong, deeply wrong, and they went too far. They crossed a line that should never have been crossed. I don't know if Rudra ever found out, but I suspect he did. And that's when everything changed."

Suresh's mind began to race. He had heard rumors about Aryan's behavior, but he had never imagined that the events in Goa would be linked to the murders. His gut twisted with unease. What the MLA was revealing sounded like the beginning of a twisted chain of events. Could this be the reason behind the killings?

MLA Sahab's voice faltered as he continued, his face darkening with regret. "Rudra's wife was devastated. She was a proud woman, but the humiliation of what happened—what Aryan and his friends did—it shattered her. And Aryan never mentioned it again. But, Inspector... I believe this is when everything started to spiral. My son and his friends were involved in something terrible, and I think Rudra may have taken matters into his own hands."

The words hung heavily in the room. The weight of the revelation seemed to suffocate the air between them. Suresh's mind spun as he tried to process this new information. Could this really be the motive behind the murders? Could the celebrated writer, Rudra, whose works were filled with intrigue and romance, now be behind these brutal killings?

He cleared his throat, his voice steady but his mind unsettled. "Are you saying that Rudra could be the one behind these murders?" he asked, his words feeling more like a statement than a question.

MLA Sahab nodded slowly, his gaze unwavering. "It's a possibility. Think about it, Inspector. The pattern of the murders—it mirrors what happened in Goa. The boys, the connection to Rudra's wife, the idea of betrayal and revenge. Everything points to him. Who else could it be?"

Suresh felt his pulse quicken as the realization began to settle in. He had always suspected that the murders were not just random acts of violence, but this new twist—this revelation about Rudra's involvement—took the case in a completely different direction. Was Rudra truly capable of such dark revenge? Was he the one pulling the strings behind the gruesome deaths? Or was there something more to this story that Suresh hadn't uncovered yet?

The complexity of the case was suffocating. Every new revelation seemed to blur the lines between victim and perpetrator. Rudra, who had once seemed like an innocent bystander, was now at the center of it all. His actions, driven by betrayal and rage, could be the reason why the boys were dying. But there was still something Suresh couldn't put his finger on. Something felt off, like there was a missing piece that could turn everything on its head.

With a deep breath, Suresh stood up, his mind reeling with the implications of what he had just heard. The case was no longer just about solving murders. It was about navigating a maze of lies, betrayals, and secrets that ran deeper than he could have imagined.

"I need to speak with Rudra," Suresh said quietly, his voice more resolute than before. "I need to know the truth."

MLA Sahab stood as well, his face a mask of worry. "Inspector, be careful. This is more than just a case now. If Rudra is indeed behind these murders, you're walking into the heart of darkness."

Suresh nodded grimly. "I'm already in it, sir."

As he left the mansion, Suresh couldn't shake the feeling that the truth was slipping through his fingers. With each passing moment, the case grew more dangerous, the stakes higher. The more he uncovered, the more it seemed like he was being pulled deeper into a web of deceit and revenge that he might never escape.

The storm inside his mind mirrored the weather outside. Dark clouds gathered overhead, and as Suresh walked through the gates of MLA Sahab's mansion, he couldn't help but feel the weight of the investigation pressing down on him. He was no longer just solving a case—he was chasing ghosts, and those ghosts were pulling him into a world of darkness from which he might never return.

Conclusion – End Of Volume 1

As Suresh walked away from MLA Sahab's mansion, his mind was a storm of confusion and frustration. The pieces of the puzzle had become more tangled, the truth more elusive than ever. The possibility that Rudra was behind the murders now hung over him like a dark cloud. But even that truth felt incomplete.

What if Rudra wasn't the only one pulling the strings? What if there was someone else in the shadows, manipulating the events, pushing everyone toward the inevitable conclusion?

With no clear answers, and with the weight of the investigation heavier than ever, Suresh knew that the coming days would test him in ways he couldn't yet comprehend. Would he be able to uncover the truth before it was too late? Or was he already too far down the rabbit hole, lost in the darkness?

The first chapter of this investigation had come to an end, but Suresh knew that the real journey had just begun. The truth was still out there, waiting to be discovered—but it was no longer clear who the hunter was and who the hunted had become.

And so, the mystery deepened, leaving Inspector Suresh to question everything he thought he knew.

End of Volume 1